Sparklebeam's Holiday Adventure

For Lily and Rhys

Special thanks to Elizabeth Galloway

ORCHARD BOOKS

First published in Great Britain in 2020 by The Watts Publishing Group

1 3 5 7 9 10 8 6 4 2

Text copyright © Working Partners Limited 2020
Illustrations © Orchard Books 2020
Series created by Working Partners Limited

A CIP catalogue record for this book is available from the British Library.

ISBN 978 1 40835 710 1

Printed and bound in Great Britain by Clays Ltd, Elcograf S.p.A.

The paper and board used in this book are made from wood from responsible sources.

Orchard Books
An imprint of Hachette Children's Group
Part of The Watts Publishing Group Limited
Carmelite House
50 Victoria Embankment
London EC4Y 0DZ

An Hachette UK Company
www.hachette.co.uk
www.hachettechildrens.co.uk

Unicorn Magic

Sparklebeam's Holiday Adventure

Daisy Meadows

ORCHARD

Contents

Story One:

A Surprise Trip

Story Two:
A Sandy Scrape

Story Three:
Holiday Heatwave!

Meet the Characters

Aisha and Emily are best friends from Spellford Village. Aisha loves sports, whilst Emily's favourite thing is science. But what both girls enjoy more than anything is visiting Enchanted Valley and helping their unicorn friends who live there.

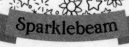

Sparklebeam

Sparklebeam uses her special magic to make sure everyone who visits Holiday Island has a wonderful time. Her three lockets are filled with the magic of the sun, sea and sand.

When Captain Prism spreads his wings, he can cast magical rainbows that form bridges to transport the creatures of Enchanted Valley from place to place!

Captain Prism

Queen Aurora

Queen Aurora is the queen of Enchanted Valley and in charge of friendship; there's nothing more important than her friends. She has a silver crown, and a beautiful coat which can change colour.

Selena is a wicked unicorn who will do anything to become queen of Enchanted Valley. She'll even steal the magical lockets if she has to. She won't give them back until the unicorns crown her queen.

Selena

Enchanted Cottage

Golden Palace

An Enchanted Valley lies a twinkle away,
Where beautiful unicorns live, laugh and play
You can visit the mermaids, or go for a ride,
So much fun to be had, but dangers can hide!

Your friends need your help – this is how you know:
A keyring lights up with a magical glow.
Whirled off like a dream, you won't want to leave.
Friendship forever, when you truly believe.

Story One

★·∴·∴·★★★★★★·∴·∴·★

A Surprise Trip

Chapter One
A Holiday in Enchanted Valley

"Get ready, Emily – here comes a big wave!" cried Aisha Khan. She was lying face-down on her surfboard, gripping the edge. As the wave came towards her, Aisha leaped to her feet. She balanced carefully, ready to ride the wave as it lifted up her surfboard …

Emily Turner, Aisha's best friend,
grinned up at her. She was lying on her
surfboard too, but the girls weren't really
in the sea – they were in the living room
of Enchanted Cottage, where Aisha lived
with her parents. Both girls were giddy
with excitement, because their families
were going on holiday together! Outside,
their parents were packing suitcases and

beach towels into the Khans' car. Soon they would set off for the coast, where they were to stay in a seaside cabin. But it was pouring with rain, and their parents were wearing anoraks over their summer clothes.

"I hope it doesn't rain while we're on holiday," said Aisha.

"Me too," said Emily. She copied Aisha, jumping up so she was standing on her board.

"Nice one!" Aisha said. "You did it perfectly. That move's called a pop up."

"I can't wait to try it for real!" said Emily.

"I'll show you lots more surf moves when we get there," Aisha said. "We can

swim, too."

"And explore the rockpools," added Emily. "And eat fish and chips! And ..."

Emily gasped, and pointed to where their suitcases stood by the living-room door. Clipped to the handles were the girls' special, unicorn-shaped keyrings. And they were glowing!

Aisha looked at Emily, her eyes shining. Both girls knew what this meant – Queen Aurora was calling for them! Aurora was a unicorn who ruled over Enchanted Valley, a world filled with all sorts of magical creatures. It was the girls' special secret, and they'd had lots of amazing adventures there with their unicorn friends.

"I wonder why Queen Aurora needs us," said Emily. "I hope Selena isn't causing trouble again." Selena was a nasty unicorn who thought she should be queen instead of Aurora – and would do anything to get her way!

"If she is, we'll do our best to stop her," Aisha said fiercely.

"Definitely," agreed Emily.

They unclipped their keyrings from the suitcases, and glanced through the window. Their parents were still busy with the luggage, so they wouldn't see what happened next – and the girls knew no time passed while they were in Enchanted Valley, so they wouldn't miss a moment of their holiday! Tingles of excitement ran through them, like the delicious, shivery feeling of eating cold ice cream. Smiling at each other, they touched the horns of their unicorn keyrings together …

Swooooosh! Blue, green and white sparkles swirled around the girls. They felt their feet leave the living-room carpet, and a breeze whipped their hair and their clothes. Then the sparkles started to fade and the girls gently drifted down again, so they were standing on lush green grass in warm sunshine. They were back in Enchanted Valley!

Holding hands, Aisha and Emily ran

across the grass. Before them stood Queen
Aurora's golden palace. Climbing roses
covered the walls, filling the air with
their sweet scent. Magnificent turrets,
like twisted unicorn horns, stood at each
corner of the palace, glinting under the
cornflower-blue sky.

Standing on the drawbridge was a tall

unicorn wearing a delicate silver crown. Her coat shimmered with the colours of a sunrise – fiery reds, warm oranges and soft pinks. She lowered her elegant horn to greet the girls.

"Queen Aurora!" cried Emily and Aisha together, and threw their arms around her long neck in a hug.

"It's lovely to see you, girls," Aurora said. Her voice was sweet and low. "Welcome back!"

Around Aurora's neck was a beautiful locket. Inside it, two

tiny suns circled together, as if they were playing. Every unicorn had a locket and the responsibility of looking after something special in Enchanted Valley. The girls knew that Aurora's friendship locket gave her the magic she needed to take care of all the friendships in Enchanted Valley.

"It's so nice to be here again," said Emily. "But why did you summon us, Aurora? Has Selena done something bad?"

Queen Aurora shook her head, making her mane swirl around her. "Oh, no! Enchanted Valley is safe and sound, I'm very glad to say." Her eyes danced. "I called you here today to give you a

special invitation. How would you like a trip to one of my favourite places in the kingdom: Holiday Island?"

"Really?" Aisha cried. She jumped around in excitement.

"That sounds amazing!" said Emily, and gave Aurora another hug.

Aurora laughed. "You'll have a wonderful time. Sparklebeam, the Holiday Island Unicorn, has invited you to stay overnight, to make it a proper holiday."

"What about you, Aurora?" Aisha asked. "Can you come, too?"

Aurora brushed her nose against Aisha's cheek fondly. "I must stay here today because I have so much royal paperwork

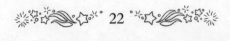

to attend to. But I'll join you tomorrow."

A sound carried towards them on the gentle breeze. *Toooooot! Toot, toot, toooooot!*

"That's the horn of the *Mint Choc Ship*," explained Queen Aurora. "It's the boat that will take you and the other holidaymakers to Holiday Island. It's about to depart!"

Aisha gave a groan of dismay. "But we'll never get to the shore in time," she said. "We'll miss the boat – and miss our holiday!"

Chapter Two
All Aboard!

"Don't worry, girls," Queen Aurora said. "No one is late for the *Mint Choc Ship*!"

Before Aisha and Emily could ask what she meant, a beautiful beam of rainbow light shot across the sky. The end curved down towards them, and landed on the ground in front of the girls' feet. It was

wide and gently sloping, like a bridge.
They gazed at it in wonder.

"The rainbow will take you to the
boat," Aurora said. "But you can't go on
holiday without luggage!"

She waved her horn, and a shower of
pink sparks swirled around it. With a
flash, two suitcases appeared beside the
girls, a shimmering ticket sitting atop
each one with the girls' names printed
clearly on them.

"Keep those safe," Queen Aurora told them. "Now step on to the rainbow – and have fun!"

Emily went first. She placed one foot on to the shimmering rainbow – and, to her amazement, it was solid! Aisha stepped up beside her. The rainbow began to move, carrying them forwards and up. "Wow!" cried Aisha, giggling in delight.

They waved down at Queen Aurora. Soon they had left her and the palace far behind, as the rainbow carried them up through the sky, over flower-sprinkled meadows, and down towards the coast. The sand was white, and the sun flashed on the waves. Bobbing on the water was a chocolate-brown boat with pale green sails decorated with polka dots.

"It looks just like mint chocolate chip ice cream," said Emily, pointing. "It must be the *Mint Choc Ship*!"

They moved down towards the deck. As they got closer, they saw that the rainbow was shining from the outstretched wings of a parrot! He had rainbow-coloured feathers and wore a sailor's hat. Other holidaymakers were already on board the ship – a group of

monkeys wearing matching sunhats, and
some pufflebunnies who were playing
catch. The boat was buzzing with excited
chatter.

When the girls had wheeled their
suitcases down on to the deck, the parrot
lowered his wings and the rainbow
vanished. "Ahoy there!" he squawked.
"Welcome aboard! I'm Captain Prism."

"Captain Prism …" said Emily thoughtfully. "Oh, I read about prisms in one of my science books! They're glass triangles that separate white light into the colours of the rainbow," she told Aisha. "Your name suits you, Captain Prism!"

The parrot ruffled his feathers happily. "Thank you! Please could you show me your tickets?" The girls did so, and Captain Prism clipped the tickets with his beak. "Attention, all holidaymakers!" he squawked. "It's time to weigh anchor,

hoist the mainsail and set our course for Holiday Island!"

The deck filled with cheers, and Emily and Aisha joined in. As the *Mint Choc Ship* pulled away from the shore, a unicorn made her way through the crowd towards them. Her coat was sandy yellow and her mane and tail were the same dazzling aqua as the sea they were sailing across. "You must be Aisha and Emily," the unicorn said. "I'm Sparklebeam, the Holiday Island Unicorn!"

"Hi, Sparklebeam!" said Emily. "Thank you very much for inviting us!"

"We can't wait to see Holiday Island," Aisha said. "What's it like?"

Sparklebeam's eyes shone. "It's a place

full of fun, where no one has anything to worry about. On the island, life is always a holiday!" The sun caught the three lockets hanging from her neck.

"They're so pretty," said Emily, leaning closer. One locket contained a tiny, blazing-bright sun. The second locket held a cute little sandcastle, and the third was full of turquoise sparkles. "And you have

three, just like our
unicorn friend
Wintertail."

"That's right!"
Sparklebeam
said. "Wintertail
is a friend of
mine too. My lockets represent the sun,
sand and sea. Together they help me
make sure Holiday Island is always the
perfect destination."

The *Mint Choc Ship* sailed on. The
other passengers were enjoying the
journey, sunbathing on the deck, and
gasping at the flying fish that leaped
above the waves. But among the happy
chatter, the girls heard a worried voice.

"My friendship fruits are probably going mouldy," it muttered. "Jumping jellyfish! How can I make potions with mouldy fruits? And I'm sure I left the kettle on …"

Emily and Aisha grinned at each other.

"That sounds like …" Aisha began.

"… Hob the goblin!" finished Emily. "Hob!" she called. "Where are you?"

A short figure standing beside the ship's mast turned around. The girls were right – it was their friend Hob! Instead of his usual gown, he wore a red shirt patterned with palm trees. Hob's wrinkly green face lit up with relief when he saw the girls.

"My dears!" he cried. "Thank goodness you're here. I'm not sure about this

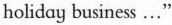

holiday business ..."

"But why not, Hob?" Aisha asked. "Holidays are fun!"

"I miss my cave," Hob said sadly. "I miss being busy with my potions." The boat swayed, and he turned a brighter shade of green. "And I miss being on dry land!"

Sparklebeam nuzzled Hob with her soft nose. "We'll be there soon," she told him. "And you deserve a holiday, Hob, because you work so hard. I promise you'll enjoy yourself!"

A bolt of lightning shot across the blue sky, startling everyone on board. Thunder rolled like waves crashing on rocks, and with a flash, a silver unicorn appeared. Her purple eyes gleamed wickedly and she stamped her powerful hooves on the deck.

"Oh no," cried Emily. "It's Selena!"

Chapter Three
Sea Rescue

A great gasp went up on the *Mint Choc Ship*. Emily heard one of the pufflebunnies whimpering with fright as they hopped as far away as they could get from Selena.

Sparklebeam stepped in front of the silver unicorn. "You'd better leave,"

she said sternly. "I won't let you spoil everyone's holiday!"

Selena scowled. "Oh, so this lot get to have a holiday, do they?" she snapped. "What about me? No one needs a holiday more than I do. Do you have any idea how exhausting it is, coming up with wicked plots and plans all the time?"

Aisha folded her arms. "Well, how

about you *stop* coming up with nasty plans, then?"

"Yeah," added Emily. "Then you'll be really well rested and relaxed."

Selena snorted. "Nice try," she said. "I'm going to have a proper holiday – on Holiday Island! I'm taking it for myself!"

Horrified gasps echoed around the deck.

"I'm going to sunbathe, and make spooky sandcastles, and turn all the ice cream to vinegar and onion flavour, and eat as much of it as I like!" Selena said gleefully. "And none of you are welcome!"

Aisha clenched her fists. "We won't let you, Selena!"

Emily shook her head. "We'll stop—"

"MONKEY OVERBOARD!" Captain
Prism's squawk rang out.

The girls and Sparklebeam rushed to
the side of the boat. In the water was
a little orange-furred monkey! He was
splashing with his paws, his tail thrashing
about. "H-h-help!" he spluttered. "I can't
swim!"

"Don't worry!" Sparklebeam called.

"We'll rescue you! Hurry, someone fetch a life ring!"

Aisha grabbed a rubber ring from the deck and was about to throw it to the monkey, when Selena knocked into her. Aisha stumbled and dropped the rubber ring as Selena barged past. Lightning flashed around Selena's horn, and she aimed it at Sparklebeam's three lockets.

Fizzzz! With a crackle of silver sparks, the lockets vanished. Two of them reappeared around Selena's

neck, and the third hung from the tip of her horn!

The girls looked in horror from the stolen lockets to the monkey struggling in the water, but they knew what they had to do.

"We have to help him!" cried Emily. "We can worry about the lockets after!"

Aisha ran and picked up the rubber ring from where it had fallen. She held it above her head, like she was on the football pitch doing a throw-in, and lobbed it into the water.

The girls held their breath. Captain Prism hopped about anxiously. Sparklebeam's forehead furrowed with worry. But then the monkey started to

swim! He circled
around the rubber
ring in a neat
backstroke, then
dived under and
re-emerged in the centre of the ring. He
clambered up and lay across it, his front
paws tucked behind his head. He grinned
up at them.

"Hee hee hee!" he squealed, holding his
belly as he laughed gleefully. "You fell for
my joke! That was so funny!" Then, using
his tail as a paddle, he sailed away.

"He tricked us!" cried Aisha. "Why
would he do that?"

"Chortle is a clever monkey," said
Selena. "Very funny, too. I might even let

him visit me on Holiday Island."

"He's helping you!" Emily frowned in annoyance. "He distracted us so you could steal Sparklebeam's lockets!"

"And it worked!" said Selena. Her eyes glittered. "Now say goodbye to the lockets and Holiday Island for good!"

Selena tossed the locket on the end of her horn into the sea. The girls watched it sink out of sight under the waves.

Cackling to herself, Selena leaped into the air, and with another bolt of lightning she disappeared.

Immediately, the *Mint Choc Ship* began to rock from side to side. The holidaymakers cried out in fright and grabbed on to the masts and the railings.

"I knew I shouldn't have come on holiday!" wailed Hob.

The sea around the boat was churning. Waves slapped the sides, growing higher and higher.

"That must have been my sea locket that Selena threw into the water," said

Sparklebeam. "Oh, girls! If we don't get it back, the sea will stay like this. We're all in terrible danger!"

Chapter Four
Waves!

"We'll get your locket back, Sparklebeam," said Emily. "We promise!"

But the girls exchanged a worried glance. How would they find a tiny locket in the huge, deep sea?

"Floundering flatfish!" yelped Hob, as the *Mint Choc Ship* lurched violently to

one side. The holidaymakers shrieked
and held on tight. Aisha, Emily, and
Sparklebeam gripped the railing. The sea
swelled beneath them, making the boat
bob up and down like they were on a
roller coaster.

"Ahoy!" squawked Captain Prism. "Big
wave to starboard!"

"Starboard?" squeaked a pufflebunny,
her ears trembling. "Where's that?"

"On the right!" called Emily,
remembering a book she'd read about a
sea voyage.

The huge wave crashed into the right
side of the boat. Salty water sprayed
across the deck, drenching the girls.

"Another wave!" Captain Prism

squawked. "Port!"

"That means left!" Emily yelled. The
wave splashed over them. Emily spat out
a mouthful of water. "Urgh!"

"We can't take much more of this," said
Aisha, pushing her soaking hair out of her
eyes. "We've got to get everyone off the
boat before it capsizes!"

Sparklebeam nodded. Her mane was

dripping wet. "But how?"

"Captain Prism's rainbow!" cried Emily. She turned to where the parrot was perched on a mast, struggling to catch the ropes that had been torn free by the waves. "Captain," she called, "could you make a rainbow to get everyone to shore?"

"A fine idea, shipmate!" Captain Prism replied. He hopped down from the mast. Gripping the deck with his claws to brace

himself against the waves, he opened his wings and swooped up. A huge rainbow beamed out of his wings, arcing up through the sky like a rocket. It touched down on the distant shore of Enchanted Valley.

Another wave hit the boat, making the rainbow rock too. "We'd better check it's safe to walk on," said Aisha. "I'll go first …"

"Be careful," said Sparklebeam.

She and Emily watched anxiously as Aisha stepped on to the rainbow. It was much wobblier than it had been in front of Queen Aurora's palace, but she was able to stay upright. She took another step, then another, climbing higher and higher.

"I think it'll work!" Aisha called back to the deck. Then her eye was caught by something glinting on the crest of one of the waves. "The locket!" she cried. "I can see it!"

"Aisha, look out!" shrieked Emily.

Aisha spun round. Another huge wave was surging across the sea – straight towards the rainbow. It looked like a wall of water was thundering towards her!

Before it could strike, she leaped off the rainbow in a dive, and plunged into the sea.

Emily gasped with horror. The wave smashed the rainbow into colourful pieces, which tumbled into the water. She peered over the side of the boat, looking for any sign of Aisha. Her heart was thumping.

"Aisha!" she called. "Are you OK?!"

Sparklebeam and Captain Prism stood on either side of Emily, searching too.

 With a
splutter, Aisha
reappeared. She
was clinging on
to a long piece
of the broken
rainbow. "I'm all right!" Aisha called. She
clambered on to the rainbow piece.

"Swim towards the ship and we'll pull you
back in!" Emily cried.

But a grin spread across Aisha's face. She
suddenly had a better idea. "This is just like
a surfboard! I can surf the waves to get to
the locket!"

"Brilliant!" Emily called back. "You
mustn't go alone, Aisha. I'll come with you!"
Then her face fell. "Oh, but I've never surfed

properly before."

"Don't worry," Aisha replied. "I'll show you what to do, just like in Enchanted Cottage!" She paddled the rainbow back towards the boat, rising and falling on the waves. "This board is big enough for both of us! I can steer while you grab the locket."

Sparklebeam gave a cry. "Look, girls! There's the locket again!" It was swirling on top of the sea, some distance from the *Mint Choc Ship*.

Nerves zoomed around Emily's tummy, like the flying fish they'd seen earlier. But she clambered over the railing, and jumped into the water.

Chapter Five
Surfing Rainbows

Aisha grabbed Emily's hand, pulling her up on to the rainbow surfboard. The two girls were lying side by side, their feet paddling in the water. The sea flung the locket up into the air, then it fell and was swept up by another wave.

"Paddle really hard, Emily!" cried

Aisha. She dipped her arm into the water, using it like a ship's rudder to steer them towards the locket. The sea tossed the rainbow board about. The girls clung on, but they didn't seem to be getting closer to the locket. "We need to pop up!" Aisha said. "Do you remember how to do it?"

"Um, I think so," said Emily. Her nerves were fluttering again.

"I know you'll be great," said Aisha. "Let's do it together! One, two, three …

pop up!"

Both girls leaped up so they were standing on the board. They stretched out their arms for balance as it skimmed over the waves, picking up speed and sending a spray of water shooting behind them. Emily let out a whoop of excitement.

"You did it, Emily!" cheered Aisha.

The two girls balanced carefully on the board, leaning one way and then the other to steer them towards the locket. They whizzed closer and closer,

turning to follow as the locket danced from wave to wave. At last they caught up with it. Emily reached out, her arm straining … she caught the chain, but the water snatched it from her fingers!

Gritting her teeth with determination, she lay down on the board and scooted forward, reaching into the water. Aisha held her legs as she stretched out – and grabbed the locket!

"Yes!" both girls cried.

The girls looked around. Not far away was

a beach of golden sand and palm trees.

Emily put the locket around her neck
to keep it safe, and Aisha leaned to
the side to steer the rainbow surfboard
towards the island. The waves tossed the
girls around but because of Aisha's skilful
surfing, they made it.

Jumping off the board, the girls waded
up on to the beach. The water sloshed
around their legs. Although choppy, it
was warm and beautifully blue. They
both pulled off their wet sandals, and
walked on the soft golden sand.

"Wow," breathed Aisha. "This is
amazing!"

"I'm so glad you think so," said
Sparklebeam as she landed on the sand

beside the girls.
Emily took off
the locket, and
Sparklebeam
lowered her head
so she could slip
it around the
unicorn's neck.
Inside it, the
turquoise sparkles shimmered.

Immediately, Sparklebeam's power to
look after the sea returned. The waves
stopped crashing, the surface of the sea
becoming smooth. Sparklebeam's eyes
shone with happiness.

"Here come the others!" said Emily.

The *Mint Choc Ship* was sailing

towards the shore – and the girls
could already hear the cheers of the
holidaymakers! When the boat reached
the shallows, Captain Prism opened his
wings once more to make a rainbow
gangplank. All the passengers walked
down it on to the beach, carrying their
luggage and thanking the girls for saving
them. Hob hurried down, clutching the

girls' suitcases. He still looked greener than usual.

"Thank you, Hob!" said Aisha, taking the cases.

Hob threw himself down on the sand. "Dry land at last!" he cried. "Oh, my dears. I really don't think holidays are for me."

"Don't worry, Hob," said Sparklebeam. "You'll have a wonderful time on Holiday Island – I promise!"

Aisha and Emily shared a worried glance. The holidaymakers had all made it safely to the island, but the girls knew they still had to find Sparklebeam's two missing lockets – or no one would have a wonderful holiday ever again!

Story Two

A Sandy Scrape

Chapter One
Welcome to Holiday Island!

"Emily, you've got to taste this!" said
Aisha. She passed Emily her mango
and passion fruit smoothie, which was
decorated with a tiny paper parasol.

Emily took a sip. "Yum!" she said, her
mouth dancing with the tangy flavours.
"Try mine – it's coconut and raspberry!"

The girls and Sparklebeam were standing outside the Smoothie Shack on the shore of Holiday Island. A flamingo was mixing up drinks for the holidaymakers, who were relaxing on the beach. Parrots flew around with baskets of fruit hanging from their beaks, offering them to the tourists. An iguana with shiny green scales was organising a game of beach volleyball, and some sloths were very, very slowly carrying everyone's suitcases up to the treehouses where the visitors would be sleeping.

Aisha gave a contented sigh. "This is the best place I've ever been to on holiday!"

"Me too," said Emily. "It's just a shame that Selena wants to spoil it for everyone."

The girls had found the locket that protected the sea, but Sparklebeam's sun and sand lockets were still missing.

"We'd better start searching for the other two lockets," Aisha said. She gave her empty glass to a flamingo waiter. "Thank you, that was delicious!"

"Come and see your room first," said Sparklebeam. She pointed her horn at the girls' clothes, which were still wet from their surfing adventure on the rough seas. "You can get changed so you're ready for whatever happens next!"

Aisha and Emily followed her up a wooden ramp to one of the treehouses. Vines of tropical flowers grew around the balcony, which had a water slide leading

straight into a lagoon below. Sparklebeam
nudged open the door, and the girls
gasped as they stepped into a room
that felt just like being in the rainforest!
The walls were painted with plants and
butterflies, and the two beds had flower-
shaped pillows. A sloth was placing the

girls' suitcases beside the beds.

"Wel … come … to … Holi … day … Island," the sloth said, very slowly. "I hope … you … have … a … love … ly … stay!"

"Thank you!" the girls said together.

The sloth left and Emily and Aisha opened their suitcases – and flower-shaped sparkles flew out of them! To the girls' amazement, their wet clothes were instantly hanging up to dry, and they were dressed in swimming costumes!

"They're magical suitcases!" said Emily with a grin. "We should have guessed that Queen Aurora wouldn't give us ordinary luggage!"

Her swimming costume had a banana

pattern, while Aisha's had a pineapple print. They were both wearing flip-flops and big straw sunhats too.

The girls and Sparklebeam went out on to the balcony. Together, they gazed down at the view of the lagoon, and beyond to the golden sand of the beach. The laughter of the other holidaymakers drifted up, and a gentle breeze wafted

coconut and mango scents around them.

"It's easy to forget that we've got a serious job to do," said Emily.

Sparklebeam smiled at them both. "That can wait," she said. "Everything's fine. See?"

"You're right," said Aisha. "We can relax for— Hey! What's that on the beach?"

Emily and Sparklebeam looked in the direction Aisha was pointing. Something very tiny was glinting brightly in the sunshine.

"Maybe it's one of the lockets!" cried Emily. "Let's go!"

Perhaps this time they'd get the locket back easily ...

Chapter Two
The Flying Locket

Aisha and Emily started to hurry back down the wooden ramp.

"Wait, girls!" called Sparklebeam. "There's a quicker way ..." She pointed her horn towards the water slide at the end of the balcony.

"Of course!" cried Aisha. She and Emily

ran back up the
ramp, and Aisha
sat on the slide and
pushed herself off.
"Whoooo!" she
cried, as she whizzed
down, down, down
in a stream of
water. The slide
tipped her
out into

the lagoon.

Emily flew out of the slide after her, laughing. "That beats walking!" she said. Sparklebeam shot out of the slide next, shaking water droplets from her mane. The girls retrieved their sunhats, which were floating on top of the lagoon's clear blue water, and swam to the edge. They climbed out on to the golden sand of the beach.

"Now to get that locket!" said Aisha.

They hurried along the beach, past a

mother phoenix and her chicks. "Look, it's
Ember and her family!" Emily said. The
girls had met the phoenix family during
one of their adventures. "Hi, Ember!"

"Hi, girls! Hi, Sparklebeam!" Ember
replied.

Emily crouched down to admire the
sandcastle the chicks were making. It had

eight turrets and was decorated with tiny pink stones. "Oh!" said Emily. "You've made Queen Aurora's palace!" The chicks cheeped happily.

They continued on their way.

"Look!" Aisha said, pointing ahead to something that glittered like a silver seashell. "It really is the locket!"

Emily followed Aisha's gaze and saw that her friend was right! The locket was lying close to some brightly painted wooden beach huts.

"Well, that was easy!" said Aisha, reaching down to pick up the locket. The tiny sandcastle gleamed inside it.

But before Aisha's fingers could touch the locket, it flew up into the air, then flopped back down on to the sand a little way away.

Aisha frowned. "That was weird! Maybe a breeze moved it."

Emily shook her head, looking up at the still palm trees. "There's no wind." She ran across the sand. But when she bent down to grab the locket, it moved again!

"Hey, come back!" called Aisha, running after it. The locket zipped along the sand, whizzing this way and that. It was heading towards a familiar green

figure sitting in a deckchair in front of one of the beach huts. "Hob!" Aisha called. "Catch that locket!"

Hob threw down his copy of *Potions Weekly* magazine, jumped up and reached for the locket. But it flew through his fingers! He tried again, but he tripped over a parasol and landed face-down on the beach. "Spppfff! Plllfffff!" Hob spluttered, spitting out a mouthful of sand.

The girls and Sparklebeam rushed to help him up. "Poor Hob," Aisha whispered to Emily. "This won't help convince him that holidays are fun …"

"Are you all right, Hob?" Sparklebeam asked, as the girls brushed sand from his colourful shirt.

"Thank you, my dears, yes," Hob said.
"But this wouldn't have happened in my
lovely cave. No sand there …"

"Hee hee hee! Ha ha ha!"

The girls and Sparklebeam looked
at each other, puzzled. "Who's that
laughing?" wondered Emily.

"Ha ha ha! Ho ho ho!"

Emily, Aisha and Sparklebeam followed
the sound of laughter along the line
of beach huts. Then a flash of orange
caught Aisha's eye. Sitting on top of one
of the beach huts was Chortle, Selena's
naughty monkey helper. In his paws was
a fishing rod … and dangling from the
massive hook at the end of the line was
the locket!

"It's Chortle!" Aisha cried. "And he's been playing another trick on us!"

Chapter Three
Hob Has a Sinking Feeling

Sparklebeam stamped her hoof firmly. "Give me my locket back right now, Chortle," she told the monkey.

But Chortle just carried on laughing. "Hee hee hee! Ho ho ho!" he giggled. He waved the rod, and the locket swung from side to side. "Every time you tried to get

it – ha! – I moved it with my fishing rod!
You looked so funny, trying to catch it!
Hee hee hee!"

Emily sighed. "Stealing isn't funny,
Chortle," she said.

"My trick was funny!" Chortle said. He
clutched his furry orange tummy. "It was
so funny, I think my sides might split! Ha
ha ha!" He rolled around on the beach
hut roof, shrieking with laughter.

"Well, helping Selena definitely isn't
funny," Aisha said sternly. "Do you
know how much trouble she's caused in
Enchanted Valley?"

Chortle stopped laughing and stared
at them. His grin turned into a grumpy
scowl. "Spoilsports," he grumbled. "You

wouldn't know a good joke if it bit you on the bottom." He plucked the locket from the end of the line, and tossed the fishing rod down on to the beach. Then he sniggered to himself. "Bottom! Bottom's a funny word …"

Aisha turned to Emily and Sparklebeam. "Maybe I can climb up on to the beach hut and get the locket," she suggested. "Sparklebeam, could you give me a boost up on your back?"

But before Sparklebeam could answer, a panicked cry rang out across the beach. "Help! Leaping lobsters! Someone, please help!"

The girls looked at each other in horror. "Hob!" they exclaimed at once.

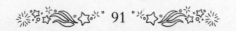 91

They ran back along the line of beach huts, Sparklebeam cantering beside them.

"Oh, no!" cried Aisha. Hob was buried up to his waist in the sand! He was wriggling around, trying to free himself, his green face scrunched up with worry.

"Oh, my dears!" Hob cried. "I don't know what's happened – my magazine blew away, and when I chased after it, I sank!" He wriggled again, but only disappeared further into the sand. Now he

was buried up to his chest!

"It's quicksand!" said Emily.

She and Aisha caught hold of Hob's hands to try to stop him slipping further.

Sparklebeam gave a whinny of dismay. "This must have happened because my sand locket is missing!" she said. "If only Chortle would give it back …"

Hob gave another wriggle. The girls both cried out in alarm as they felt the sand tugging at him. They held on to Hob's hands tightly, but the quicksand sucked him in even further. Now only his shoulders, arms and head were visible!

Hob turned a pale shade of green. "I have to say," he said, "when Captain Prism told us about the activities available on Holiday Island, he never mentioned this!"

"Oh, this is awful!" said Aisha. Tears sprang into her eyes. "Come on, we've got to dig him out!" She let go of Hob's hand and started scooping at the sand. But Hob sank again – and one of his arms disappeared!

Sparklebeam's eyes were wide with fright. "How are we going to save him?" she cried.

Chapter Four
Goblin Fishing

"Aisha, stop digging!" Emily urged her.
"Hob, stop struggling! That will make
you sink faster."

"So what can we do?" Aisha asked.

Emily frowned, trying to remember
what she knew about quicksand. "Just
stay still for now, Hob," she said.

Shouts rang out around the beach. A pair of pufflebunnies were squealing in alarm as their parasol sank into the sand, and Ember and her chicks were flapping their wings in panic. "Come back, sand palace!" cheeped one of the chicks, as their model of Queen Aurora's home disappeared.

Aisha groaned. "More quicksand!"

"Everyone, get off the beach!" called Sparklebeam. She leaped up into the air

and soared over the sand. "It isn't safe!" She touched down on to the sand so a couple of sloth waiters carrying trays of drinks could clamber on to her back, and flew them to the safe area around the lagoon. Captain Prism appeared, and gently scooped up a couple of Ember's chicks in his claws. Emily and Aisha comforted Hob, who looked like he was on the verge of tears. Other holidaymakers ran for cover, leaping and skipping over the patches of quicksand.

In a few moments, the beach was empty apart from the girls, Sparklebeam and poor Hob. Sweat was trickling down his green face.

"We're going to get you out somehow,"

Aisha promised him. "There's got to be a way …"

Emily agreed. "We need to work out how to grab hold of Hob without getting too close. Otherwise, we'll sink ourselves!" she said.

"I know!" Aisha cried. "We can use Chortle's fishing rod!"

"Great idea!" said Emily. "Let's get it!"

The girls dashed back down the line of beach huts. Emily scooped up a handful of pebbles and tossed them ahead of their path – if the pebbles sank, they knew there was a patch of quicksand there, and dodged around it.

By the time they reached the spot where Chortle had abandoned his fishing rod, only a few centimetres of it were still visible. "It's sinking, too!" said Emily. "Oh, no!"

Aisha put on a burst of speed, and sprinted over. She grabbed the fishing line, which was trailing across the beach, and pulled hard. The rod came shooting up out of the sand! Emily gave Aisha a high five and the girls ran back the way they'd come, following the trail of pebbles.

When they got there, Hob had sunk even further. Only his head and one hand were still free. "We don't have much time," said Sparklebeam, who was trembling with worry.

Her heart pounding, Aisha wound up the fishing line, then lifted the rod upright.

I've got to get this right the first time,
she thought. *Or we won't be able to save
Hob ...* Beside her, Emily was holding her
breath.

Aisha leaned back, then swung the rod
forwards. At the same time, she released
the fishing line. With a whirring sound
it spooled out from the rod, and sailed
through the air. The line landed close
enough to Hob's hand that he could
grab the thick hook
and close his fingers
around it.

"Yes!" shouted
Emily, hugging Aisha.

"Don't let
go, Hob!" said

Sparklebeam.

Emily held on to the fishing rod too, and
Sparklebeam gripped it with her teeth.
"One," said Aisha, "two, three … Pull!"

The three friends pulled back on the rod.
Aisha could feel the muscles in her arms
straining.

Sparklebeam clenched her jaw, and Emily was pulling so hard she nearly lost her balance.

But Hob didn't budge.

"Harder!" Aisha said through gritted teeth.

They yanked back on the rod. Aisha's arms were trembling, and Emily could feel the skin of her palms being rubbed painfully. Sparklebeam gave a whinny of determination and bit down so hard on the rod she left teeth marks.

Pop! Hob's shoulders came free. *Pop!* Then came his other arm, then his chest. *Pop!* In a rush, the rest of Hob shot out of the quicksand. He slithered over the beach towards them, and came to a stop at their feet.

"Startling starfish!" Hob said weakly. "That was a close one. Thank you for rescuing me!"

"Thank goodness you're safe," said Sparklebeam. "I'll fly you to the lagoon, Hob."

The girls lifted him on to the unicorn's back. Hob's lovely holiday shirt was torn, his face was smudged with dirt, and his glasses were crooked. He looked a sorry sight.

"Do you think you could fly me back to my cave?" Hob asked. "This holiday has turned into a disaster!"

The girls reached up to hug him. "It will get better once we've got Sparklebeam's lockets back," said Aisha. "We promise!"

"Can you wait until then?" asked Emily.

Hob wiped his glasses on his sleeve. "Well ..." he said. "I believe in you, my dears. If anyone can find the lockets and make Holiday Island fun again, it's you!"

"Thank you, Hob!" said Aisha. "We'll do our best!"

They waved goodbye as Sparklebeam flew him back to the treehouses.

"Right," said Aisha. "As soon as

Sparklebeam gets back, it's time to talk to Chortle – and work out how to make him give us the locket!"

Chapter Five
Chuckling Chortle

A few moments later, once Sparklebeam had returned from delivering Hob to his treehouse, Aisha and Emily climbed aboard the unicorn's back. The beach was still too full of quicksand to walk on!

"Thank you, Sparklebeam!" said Emily as she settled herself behind Aisha.

"No problem!" replied Sparklebeam. "We don't want anyone else getting stuck!"

Aisha wrapped her arms around Sparklebeam's neck, and behind her Emily held on to Aisha's waist. They flew over the sand to where Chortle was still sitting on top of the beach hut. He was twirling the locket around one of his fingers, giggling to himself. He scowled when he saw the girls and Sparklebeam.

"What do you want?" he snapped.

"The locket, of course," said Sparklebeam. "Didn't you see the quicksand, Chortle? If you don't give back the locket, someone will get hurt!"

For a second, Chortle frowned with

something that looked like concern. Then his face cleared. "Don't believe you," he said. "I think you're having a laugh." He clenched his fist around the locket.

Sparklebeam sighed, then circled away from the beach huts, so they could decide what to do. "How are we ever going to persuade him?" she wondered.

An idea was chasing through Aisha's head. "I know!" she cried. "Chortle thought we were having a laugh … What if we really did?"

Emily grinned. "You mean, tell him jokes?"

"Exactly!" said Aisha. "If we distract him, maybe we can get the locket."

"Let's try it!" agreed Sparklebeam.

She flew them back, and hovered beside Chortle's beach hut once more.

"You lot again!" Chortle said moodily. "Go away." He turned around so he was sitting with his back to them.

"Hey, Chortle," said Aisha. "Where do sharks go on holiday?"

Chortle shrugged.

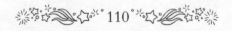

"Finland!" Aisha said. "Get it?"

"Not funny," said Chortle — but his shoulders were shaking, as if he was trying not to laugh.

"Tell another one!" whispered Sparklebeam.

"Chortle," said Emily, "what happens if you wear a watch on an aeroplane?"

The monkey peered at her over his shoulder. "I don't know," he said. "What happens?"

"Time flies!" said Emily.

"Ha!" shrieked Chortle. "Time flies! Good one!" Then he clapped his paws over his mouth to stop his giggles. The locket dangled from one of his paws.

Emily and Aisha glanced at each other

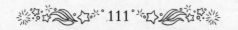

hopefully. *Maybe one more joke will do it*, thought Aisha.

"Chortle, what's brown and hairy, and wears sunglasses?" she asked.

"I don't know!" Chortle said. "Tell me!" He bounced up and down on his paws.

"A coconut on holiday."

Chortle threw back his head and let out a burble of laughter. "Hee hee hee! Ha ha ha! Ho ho ho! A coconut ... on holiday!" He scampered around the beach hut roof, then slapped it with delight. "Ha ha ha!"

The locket flew from his paw. It sailed through the air.

Chortle stopped laughing and gave an angry screech. He snatched at the locket, but missed, and had to balance with his tail to stop himself falling off the hut.

Sparklebeam turned sharply, chasing after the locket. Aisha clung to her mane with one hand and stretched out the other, like a goalkeeper – and her fingers closed around the locket!

"Good save!" said Emily, patting Aisha on the back.

"No!" shrieked Chortle, and bounded away, swinging through the trees behind the huts.

Aisha slipped the locket around Sparklebeam's

long neck. Immediately, objects popped up all over the beach from where they'd been swallowed by the quicksand. Hob's deckchair shot up, and colourful parasols and stripy towels sprang to the surface. Even the sand palace made by Ember's chicks reappeared.

Sparklebeam touched down, and the girls jumped from her back on to the soft, warm sand. "Thank you, girls," the unicorn said, nuzzling them each in turn. "You've saved the beach!"

"We did it together," said Emily, as she
and Aisha hugged her.

The sun was low in the sky now,
dipping down towards the sea.

"Here comes the sunset!" said
Sparklebeam, as the sun sank down to
the horizon. "Holiday Island sunsets are
beautiful, just you watch."

The girls waited, holding their breath.

But then the sun dropped out of sight.
Instead of a beautiful display of light,
Holiday Island was plunged into gloomy,

swirling, dingy darkness.

"Oh no!" cried Aisha.

"What happened?" Emily wondered.

In the gloom the girls could just see Sparklebeam, who hung her head. "It must be because my sun locket is still missing," the unicorn said sadly. "I'm sorry, girls."

"We'll get it back tomorrow," Aisha promised.

"Don't worry, Sparklebeam," said Emily. "We won't give up until Holiday Island is safe again!"

Story Three

Holiday Heatwave!

Chapter One
Boiling Breakfast

"Oof!" said Aisha, kicking the covers off her bed. "I'm so hot!"

"Me too," said Emily, reaching for a book and fanning herself with the pages.

The girls had just woken up in their treehouse room. Sunshine streamed on to the decorated walls, making the colours extra bright. Aisha got up with a stretch, and opened the window. The air that wafted in was even warmer!

She turned to Emily with a worried frown. "It's already boiling out there," she said.

Both girls knew why – because their friend Sparklebeam was still missing the sun locket. Selena had it now and she was controlling the sun – that's why the sunset had been so ugly last night, and that must be why it was too hot now. Aisha and Emily had already rescued Sparklebeam's sea and sand lockets, but if they couldn't get back the sun locket too, horrible Selena would be able to take over the island and spoil it for everyone else.

"Let's go down to breakfast," said Emily, jumping out of bed. "We need to start searching before it gets even hotter!"

The girls washed then opened the magical suitcases Queen Aurora had given them. They couldn't help grinning as flower-shaped sparkles flew out of the cases. In a moment, their pyjamas were neatly folded on their pillows. Emily now wore green shorts and a T-shirt with an ice cream motif, while Aisha's T-shirt was decorated with seahorses and her shorts were blue.

"Cool!" they

both said together. On their feet were comfy sandals, and they wore straw sunhats.

Hand in hand, the girls walked down the wooden ramp, then along a pathway edged with mango trees to a café called The Breakfast Bar. The café was outside, and had flower-shaped tables shaded by parasols. But despite this, the holidaymakers sitting there already looked far too hot. Ember the phoenix was using her wings to fan her little chicks.

"It's too hot even for us phoenixes!" exclaimed Ember.

From one of the tables, the girls' friend Hob the goblin was waving at them.

Aisha and Emily went to join him.

"Morning, Hob!" said Aisha, as they sat down. "How did you sleep?"

"Terribly!" said Hob, dabbing his sticky green face with his handkerchief. "I was sweating through my sheets. Oh, my dears, I do wish I was back in my nice cool cave."

A flamingo waiter brought the girls

glasses of freshly squeezed orange juice. "What would you like for breakfast?" he asked. "Our menu is anything you would like!"

"Wow, anything?" said Emily. All she wanted was something cool!

"How about ice cream?" suggested Aisha. "It's delicious and it's cold!"

The water bowed his long pink neck. "Coming right up, young ladies."

"I think you'd better have ice cream for breakfast, too, little ones," Ember told her chicks. "It's the only thing cool enough to eat."

"Hooray!" the chicks cheeped.

"Only for today," said Ember.

A few minutes later, the girls were tucking into ice cream sundaes topped  with chocolate chips and butterscotch sauce. But before they were even halfway through, the ice cream had turned into a sticky puddle. Hob pushed aside his plate of bread and jam. "Too hot to eat," he grumbled. "Sweltering starfish! Why didn't I go on a skiing holiday instead? I could be up a nice cold mountain right now, surrounded by snow ..."

Sparklebeam and Captain Prism came hurrying towards their table.

Sparklebeam's aqua-coloured horn flashed in the sunshine, and Captain Prism was so hot his feathers were stuck together.

"Oh, girls!" cried Sparklebeam. "Everyone is far too hot already — and it's still only early morning. No one's having a good time! Maybe we should get the *Mint Choc Ship* ready and sail everyone home."

Emily put down her spoon. "We won't let Selena ruin everyone's holiday!"

"Surely there's something else they could do," said Aisha, "until we find your locket?"

Captain Prism nodded. "How about asking all the holidaymakers to go back

to their treehouses? It's cooler inside."

Sparklebeam heaved a sigh. "That's not much fun," she said.

"We've got lots of board games," said Captain Prism, "and arts and crafts materials. And everyone can play charades and noughts and crosses."

"Well ... all right," agreed Sparklebeam. "At least everyone will be out of this scorching sun."

Captain Prism began to explain their plan to the other guests. The creatures looked disappointed, but made their way back up to their treehouse rooms.

"But girls," said Sparklebeam, "what about you? You'll get sunburned!"

For the first time during his holiday,

Hob gave a huge grin.
"My dears, I think I can
help you with that …"

Chapter Two
Sunbathing Selena

Hob reached under the café table and rummaged around in his straw beach bag. He pulled out a jar. On the label, in Hob's spidery handwriting, it said: *Super-Strength Sun Cream*.

"I made this last night, when I couldn't sleep," Hob explained. "I brought a few emergency potion ingredients with me in my suitcase. Here, try it!" He opened the jar and passed it to the girls.

"Thank you, Hob!" said Emily.

"This is just what we need!" Aisha said. She scooped out some of the sun cream and applied it all over herself. Emily did the same, then she rubbed some into Sparklebeam's muzzle and the tips of her ears.

"Now we're ready to find that locket," said Emily.

"Take the sun cream with you," said Hob, "and don't forget to keep applying it. Good luck!"

The girls and Sparklebeam set off into the centre of Holiday Island. "We didn't

spot the sun locket on the beach," said
Sparklebeam, "so I think this will be the
best place to start our search."

The further they went, the greener the
island became. They walked beneath
more palm trees, ducked under vines, and
passed enormous yellow and blue flowers
that hung like pom-poms.

They were scrambling past some bushes
with huge leaves shaped like parasols,

when Emily suddenly stopped. She put a finger to her lips.

"Can you hear that?" she whispered.

Drifting through the trees came a voice. "Ah, how I love this scorching sun! It'll keep those pesky girls away, for sure. They'll be far too hot to climb this tree and find the locket …"

Aisha gasped. "That's Selena!"

Following the sound of Selena's voice, they crept through the bushes. Emily and Aisha's hearts were fluttering like butterflies. They crouched behind a bush with purple flowers, and peered around it.

In front of them was a clearing. A cluster of palm trees stood at the edge, and beneath the tallest palm tree,

stretched out on a sun lounger, was Selena!

The wicked unicorn was wearing sunglasses shaped like lightning bolts. Beside her was a table with a glass on it, filled with a horrible-looking green liquid. Selena leaned down to slurp it up through a straw.

"Ah!" she sighed. "This is the life. Once

I've made all those silly creatures leave, this will be the perfect holiday destination. It will need a new name though …" She laughed, and lightning flickered around her long, very sharp horn. "I know – I'll call it Nightmare Island! Ha!" With one hoof, she began flipping through the pages of a magazine called *Tips and Tricks for Villains*.

The girls and Sparklebeam huddled close together. "It sounds like the locket must be up that tall palm tree," whispered Emily.

Aisha nodded. "We need to get Selena to move so we can get to it."

"But how?" wondered Sparklebeam. "Everyone else is miserable in this boiling sun, but Selena seems to love it."

Emily nodded thoughtfully. "Maybe we can put her in the shade …" Her gaze fell on the big leaves they were hiding beside. "I know!" she said. "Wait here!" She darted back the way they had come. When she reappeared, she was holding four of the big parasol-shaped leaves they'd passed earlier. "Sparklebeam," she said, "if you fly us up to the treetops, we could use these leaves to stop the sun shining on Selena."

"Great idea, Emily!" said Aisha.

The girls climbed on to Sparklebeam's back, each holding two of the leaves. Sparklebeam reared up, then took off. She flew upwards, careful to stay hidden behind the trees and bushes, until she was level with the treetops. On the ground below, the girls saw Selena slurping her green drink in the blazing sun.

"Now!" whispered Emily, hoping her plan would work …

Chapter Three
A Nasty Surprise

Emily and Aisha held up their parasol leaves. Immediately, they cast a shadow across the clearing.

"Pah!" Selena spat out her drink in surprise. "Where's the lovely scorching sun gone?" She looked up towards the girls, who ducked behind their leaves. "And

where did those annoying leaves come from?" She got up from her lounger, and looked up at the tall palm tree. "Those girls will never find the locket," she muttered to herself. "It's safe up there. I'm going to find a new patch of sun …"

She stomped away through the trees.

"It worked!" cried Aisha. "We'll soon have your locket back, Sparklebeam! Will you fly us over to the tall palm tree?"

"Of course!" said Sparklebeam. The girls

threw aside the parasol leaves and leaped on to Sparklebeam, who zoomed over to the tree. Aisha clambered into the top of the tree but Emily stayed on Sparklebeam – there wasn't room at the top of the wobbly tree for all of them, and Aisha was a better climber. The tree wavered with her weight but Aisha gripped the trunk between her knees, just as she did when she was climbing the ropes in PE class.

"It's got to be here somewhere," Aisha muttered, as she rummaged through the palm's long, feathery leaves and clusters of coconuts. But she couldn't see a glint of metal anywhere.

"No luck?" called Emily, from Sparklebeam's back. "Maybe try shaking

the tree, and see if it falls out?"

"Good idea!" said Aisha. She wrapped her arms and legs tightly around the trunk, and arched her body from side to side. The palm tree swayed – and Aisha heard a rattling sound. "What was that?"

"I think it's coming from inside one of the coconuts!" said Sparklebeam, her eyes bright.

Emily gasped. "Has Selena hidden the locket inside a coconut?"

"Only one way to find out!" said Aisha. She shook each coconut in turn. "Nothing," she said. "Nope, not that one …" But when she tested the smallest coconut of them all, it rattled! "Got it!" Aisha plucked the coconut  from the tree and held it up triumphantly.

"Oh, I'm so pleased!" said Sparklebeam. She flew round in a happy loop, making Emily giggle. "I've got all my lockets back! Holiday Island is safe from Selena again!"

"It very nearly is," said Aisha. "We've still got to get the sun locket out of the coconut." She tapped it against the palm tree's trunk. "How can we break it open?"

"Try throwing it on the ground," suggested Emily.

Aisha lobbed the coconut down to the middle of the clearing. But it bounced on a patch of flowers, and didn't break. "I'll try again!" Aisha called to the others. She had just started to scramble down the trunk, gripping it with her legs, when both Emily and Sparklebeam gave yells of alarm.

"Hurry, Aisha!" shouted Sparklebeam.

"Chortle's coming!" cried Emily.

Aisha looked down – and her heart felt like it was flipping over. Selena's naughty monkey helper was scampering on all fours towards the coconut!

Aisha scrambled down the trunk.

Sparklebeam zoomed down too and
landed. Emily leaped off. Emily, Aisha
and Sparklebeam sprinted towards the
coconut …

But Chortle was faster. "Hee hee hee!"
he sniggered, snatching the coconut up in
his paws. "The joke's on you, this time!"
And he bounded away into the trees.

"After him!" cried Emily. They got on
to Sparklebeam's back again, and she
galloped after the monkey. They followed
the sound of his giggles through the
undergrowth. Sparklebeam leaped over
fallen logs and cantered around banana

trees, until they emerged into another clearing. The girls jumped down, and the three friends walked into the clearing.

At the opposite end, three tall sticks were stuck into the ground. On top of each of them rested a coconut. A banner hanging from the branches above the coconuts read: *Chortle's Coconut Shy*. Chortle was sitting next to it, a huge grin on his furry orange face.

"Who wants to play a game?" he asked them. "It's very simple. Hit the right coconut, and the locket is yours." He rubbed his paws together gleefully. "But if you hit the wrong coconut – you'll have a surprise!"

Chapter Four
Chortle's Coconut Shy

Emily put her hands on her hips. "It looks like we don't have much choice," she said crossly. "How does this game work, Chortle?"

Chortle picked up three small balls that were lying in the grass. "You try to hit the coconuts with these," he said, still smirking. "And you – ha! – see what – hee! – happens! Ha ha ha!"

"Fine," said Aisha, taking one of the balls from him. She fixed her gaze on the coconut on the right, and narrowed her eyes. *Imagine it's a wicket*, she thought, remembering her cricket coaching. Drawing back her arm, she threw the ball.

Crack! The ball hit the coconut right in the centre.

Whoosh! But the coconut exploded – and a shower of green gunge shot out of it, covering Aisha!

Chortle rolled

around on the grass, hooting with laughter. "Surprise!" he yelled. "No locket! Ha ha ha!"

"Yuck!" cried Aisha, wiping smears of gunge from her face.

Sparklebeam stamped her hooves. "That was a mean trick, Chortle," she told him.

"It was a funny trick!" Chortle shrieked. "Hee hee hee! Who's next?"

"I guess I could try," said Emily, as Aisha tried to wipe the slippery gunge off her hands.

Emily took the next ball from Chortle. She stared hard at the coconut on the left, just as she'd seen Aisha do. Then she threw the ball.

Crack! Her shot clipped the top of the

coconut. *Whoosh!* Emily darted backwards, but it was too late – her coconut exploded, and purple gunge spurted all over her!

"Eww!" cried Emily.

"No locket!" yelled Chortle. "Ha ha ha! You're all purple!"

Sparklebeam eyed him coldly. "This still isn't funny, Chortle. At least we know the locket is in the middle coconut. Your silly game will soon be over."

Chortle was too busy laughing to respond.

Aisha had managed to clean her hands

by wiping them on the grass. "I'll do it," she said, and took the ball.

"Go, Aisha!" said Emily.

"Aim and fire!" said Sparklebeam.

Aisha concentrated on the middle coconut. The rest of the clearing seemed to melt away as she focused on her target. She raised her arm, and flung the ball …

Crack! The coconut split into pieces. Aisha leaped back – but there was no gunge this time.

She ran to the shy, and searched through the broken pieces of coconut. Emily and Sparklebeam raced to join her.

"But where's the locket?" wondered Emily, picking up an empty bit of shell.

Aisha clenched her fists. "It's not here, is

it, Chortle? That coconut was empty!"

"HA!" Chortle roared. "HA HA HA!"
He lay down and slapped the ground
with his paws. Then he stopped laughing,
and looked up at them. "But why aren't
you laughing too?"

"We've already told you," said
Sparklebeam. "It's not funny. It's just
mean."

"Really?" said Chortle. His bottom lip
wobbled. "You're not joking?"

"No," said Emily. "We're not."

Chortle's face crumpled and he started
to sob. His orange cheeks were soon wet
with tears.

Despite the monkey's horrible pranks,
the girls couldn't help feeling sorry for

him. Aisha went and
put an arm around
him, while Emily held
his paw. "What's wrong,
Chortle?" Emily asked.

"All – boo! – I want to – hoo! – do is
make – hoo! – people laugh," Chortle
told them. "But no one – boo! – likes –
hoo! – my jokes."

Sparklebeam kneeled in front of him.
"That's because they're not very nice," she
told him gently.

"They're helping Selena," said Emily.

"And she's trying to spoil Holiday
Island," finished Aisha.

"She is?" asked Chortle in surprise.

"Yes," said Sparklebeam. "Look, there

are lots of other ways you could make people laugh. I know! It would be lovely to have an entertainer living on the island, who could perform for all the holidaymakers."

"Oh, yes," said Aisha. "You could have your own comedy show!"

Chortle wiped his eyes. "Really?"

Sparklebeam smiled at him. "Really!"

Chortle got to his paws. "I could make a stage out on the beach," he said excitedly. "I've even got the perfect costume to wear! Everyone will want to come to Holiday Island to see Chortle's Chuckle Show!"

The girls and Sparklebeam laughed as he hugged them each in turn.

"Wait a second!" Chortle said. "I nearly forgot …"

He scampered off into the trees and came back with a coconut. He plucked one of the coconut-shy sticks from the ground, and used the tip to split it open. Out tumbled Sparklebeam's locket, with its tiny sun shining inside.

"I'm really sorry I took it," Chortle told them. "I didn't mean to harm Holiday Island."

"That's all right," said Sparklebeam.

Aisha and Emily grinned at each other.
They had the third and final locket!

Chapter Five
Party on the Beach

Sparklebeam leaned down, and Emily slipped the locket around her neck. It hung with her other two lockets – sea, sand and sun, back where they belonged. Immediately, the scorching hot sunshine became a lovely soft warmth.

"Thank you, girls," said Sparklebeam.

"You've saved Holiday Island! And you as well, Chortle – we needed your help." The monkey beamed with pride.

They all made their way back to the treehouses. The holidaymakers were rushing out of their rooms and down the ramps, whooping and cheering. "The island is safe!" cheered Ember, while her chicks flapped their tiny wings in delight. "Thank you, Emily and Aisha!"

The pufflebunnies had their snorkels on, ready to play in the pool. Sloths plodded around handing out brightly coloured beach towels, big smiles spreading – very slowly – on their faces. Captain Prism flew towards the girls, and wrapped them up in a feathery hug.

"I knew you could do it!" he squawked.
Then he noticed Chortle. "What in the
deep blue sea is that naughty monkey
doing here?"

The girls quickly explained how
Chortle had helped them in the end. "And
now he's going to be the Holiday Island
entertainer," said Sparklebeam.

Captain Prism let out a big squawking

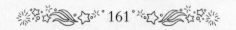

laugh. He threw his wings around Chortle. "You'll be perfect! Welcome to the Holiday Island team!"

Flamingo waiters bustled about, offering the holidaymakers trays of drinks. "Smoothies for everyone," cried one of them, "so we can toast the girls!"

"Great idea!" said Sparklebeam. "Hip, hip—"

But suddenly thunder roared around them. With a flash of lightning, Selena appeared. More lightning flickered around her horn. Her sunglasses were gone, and she glared at the holidaymakers.

"I see everyone's having a wonderful holiday," she snapped. "Everyone except me! This has been the worst holiday ever,

and it's all because of you girls!" She
stamped her heavy hooves.

"You ought to go home, then,"
Sparklebeam told her.

"Oh, I'm already going!" said Selena.
"I hate holidays, anyway. Thinking up
wicked deeds and plots is much more
my style! I can't wait to be back in my

spooky castle …"

With another flash of lightning, Selena took off and flew away over the sea.

"Thank goodness," said Sparklebeam. "Now – let's celebrate with a party!"

A short while later, everyone was at the beach. Some of the holidaymakers were dancing to a band of toucans, while others were paddling in the sea, eating ice cream or drinking more delicious fruit smoothies. Captain Prism was making tiny rainbows for the littlest guests to slide down into the sea. Ember's chicks cheeped with excitement as they shot down the slides. Aisha and Emily went to join in a game of beach volleyball, and to their surprise, the person who passed the ball to

them was Hob!

"Dancing dolphins!" he cried. "Now I know why everyone said I should go on holiday! I'm having so much fun!"

"That's brilliant, Hob!" Aisha said, passing the ball back to him.

"Oh, look," said Emily. "Chortle's about to start his show!"

The girls and Hob went to join the

crowd gathered around a small stage, where Chortle stood, wearing a sparkly top hat and waistcoat. "Ahem," he said into the microphone. "Welcome to Chortle's Chuckle

Show! So, what did the banana say to the monkey?"

"We don't know!" cried the crowd.

"Nothing," said Chortle, "because bananas can't talk!"

The crowd erupted into giggles – and the girls caught a sweet, musical laugh ringing out among them. They turned around to see Queen Aurora! Her orange, pink and red coat gleamed in the sunshine, and she bowed her horn to the girls in greeting.

"Hello, girls," Aurora said. "Hello, Hob! I heard about Selena stealing Sparklebeam's lockets," she went on. "Thank you for helping us again! I don't know what Enchanted Valley would do

without you."

"You're very welcome," said Emily.

"We'll always help our unicorn friends," said Aisha.

The party continued in a whirl of dancing, games and laughter. At last, it was time for Aisha and Emily to go home.

"Thank you for inviting us to Holiday

Island," Emily said to Sparklebeam. "We've had so much fun!"

"I have a special present for you," said Sparklebeam, nuzzling them both. She waved her horn and in a flash, two twinkling charms appeared out of thin air and dropped into the palms of their hands. When they looked, the girls could see they were golden charms in the shape of shining suns.

"So you'll never forget me," Sparklebeam said.

"Of course we'll never forget you!" the girls cried together as they hugged her goodbye.

Queen Aurora's horn glowed, and blue, green and white sparkles shimmered around the girls, as if the sea was swirling around them. Holiday Island faded away, and Emily and Aisha felt like they were flying …

When the sparkles vanished, the girls were standing in the living room of Enchanted Cottage once more. "Wow," said Aisha with a sigh. "That was an amazing adventure!"

Emily nodded. "And now we're going on holiday again!"

"I can't wait!" said Aisha. "I just wish we could pack some Holiday Island sunshine into our suitcases."

"So do— Aisha, look!" cried Emily,

pointing to the window. Outside, it was still raining, but the sun was starting to break through. And sweeping across the sky was a beautiful rainbow!

"It's like Captain Prism is saying hello," said Aisha. The girls grinned at each other.

"Aisha!" called Mrs Khan from outside. "Emily! It's time to go."

The girls picked up their surfboards and grabbed the handles of their suitcases. Their unicorn keyrings were clipped on to their suitcases again, and the shiny new sun-shaped charms caught the light beautifully. Emily and Aisha hurried out to the car, sure they were about to have the best holiday ever!

The End

Join Emily and Aisha
for another adventure in …
Queen Aurora's Birthday Surprise
Read on for a sneak peek!

"What about a new scarf?" suggested Emily Turner brightly. "Dad lost his scarf, didn't he?"

Emily's mum shook her head. "He bought himself a new one."

Aisha slurped up the last sip of her raspberry smoothie. "I know! What about a tie?"

"That's a great idea," Emily said. "But we got Dad a tie last year. Didn't we, Mum?"

"I'm afraid so," said Mrs Turner. Her forehead was creased into a worried frown. Emily and Aisha shared an anxious look across Emily's breakfast table. Her dad's birthday was only a week away, and they still hadn't come up with the perfect present!

Aisha got down from her stool and went to the sink to wash her empty glass. Emily felt a jolt of excitement as she noticed that the keyring clipped on to the waistband of Aisha's jumpsuit was glowing! She looked down at her own keyring where it lay on the table. Just like Aisha's keyring, Emily's was shaped like a unicorn – and it was glowing as well!

Emily took her glass to the sink too. As

she turned on the tap, she whispered to Aisha, "Queen Aurora is summoning us!"

Aisha grinned. Both girls knew that they were about to return to Enchanted Valley for another adventure with their unicorn friends!

"Mum," said Emily, "please can Aisha and I go to the pond? Maybe a walk will help us think of present ideas."

"Of course," said Mrs Turner. "Just make sure you're back before lunchtime."

Excitement charged through the girls like galloping ponies. They crossed the road and walked up a muddy path towards the Spellford village pond.

"I can't wait to go back to Enchanted Valley!" said Aisha. "I wonder why Queen

Aurora needs our help ... I hope Selena isn't causing trouble again!"

Enchanted Valley was a secret land full of magical creatures. The unicorns helped take care of the valley, and Queen Aurora ruled over them all with kindness and wisdom. But a horrible unicorn called Selena thought she should be queen instead – and so she kept coming up with wicked plans to take over. So far, Emily and Aisha had managed to stop her, but they knew that Selena was clever and very determined ...

Just as they'd hoped, there was no one around to see what was about to happen except for a pair of ducks paddling through the reeds. The girls took out their unicorn keyrings.

"Let's go!" Emily said with a smile.

They touched the keyrings' horns together. There was a dazzling flash, like fireworks lighting up the sky. Aisha and Emily felt their feet leave the ground. They floated up, up, up like balloons – and then their feet settled on to soft grass. The light faded.

In front of them stood Queen Aurora's magnificent golden palace. Its eight turrets, each shaped like a unicorn horn, rose up into a cloudless blue sky. Pink roses grew over the walls, and the air was sweet with their scent. The palace stood on the top of a hillside, and around it lay misty woodlands, meadows of flowers, and a river that gleamed silver in the sunshine.

"We're back in Enchanted Valley!" said Aisha. The girls hugged each other with delight.

They looked towards the shimmering moat of water that circled around the palace. Across it lay a wooden drawbridge, which led through the gates. Usually when the girls arrived in Enchanted Valley, Queen Aurora came trotting across the drawbridge to meet them.

But today the drawbridge was empty.

"That's strange," said Emily. "I wonder if—"

"Psssssst!"

Emily and Aisha looked at each other. "What was that?" asked Aisha.

"Psssssst!"

"Is someone there?" called Emily.

Then came a giggle, and a voice said, "Over here! Under the willow tree!"

The girls hurried over to a willow tree that grew beside the moat. Its long, trailing branches formed a curtain that dipped into the water. Aisha pushed the branches aside, and she and Emily stepped beneath the tree. The girls gasped. Standing there was a tall yellow unicorn, with a purple mane and tail and a blue horn. And beside her were three little unicorn foals! One was purple, one was yellow and one was blue.

The foals trotted around the girls, nuzzling against them and whinnying.

The mother unicorn laughed. "My triplets are very excited about meeting you!" she said to the girls. "We've heard so much about your adventures, you see. My name's Canterpop. Will you tell Emily and Aisha your names?" she asked her foals.

"I'm Boxie," said the purple foal. He dipped his tiny horn in greeting.

The yellow foal reared up on his hind legs, waving his little hooves. "I'm Bunting!"

The smallest foal trotted behind her mother and then leaped out suddenly. "And I'm Boo!" she shouted.

"It's lovely to meet you all," said Aisha.

Bunting cantered around them again, making the locket that hung around his neck jangle. Emily noticed that each of the three foals was wearing a locket, but Canterpop's neck was bare. "Oh!" said Emily. "Where's your locket? Selena hasn't taken it, has she?"

"No," said Canterpop. "Thank goodness! I've lent them to my triplets! I look after everything to do with parties and celebrations in Enchanted Valley, and my lockets are for presents, decorations and surprises. But today I've given them to Boxie, Bunting and Boo. They aren't old enough for their own lockets yet, but—"

"But we've got a plan, haven't we, Mum?" said Boxie. He swished his purple tail excitedly. He wore a locket with a wrapped present in it.

"It's a really good plan!" said Bunting, whose locket contained a big balloon.

Boo looked out from behind Canterpop. "It's Queen Aurora's birthday tomorrow!" Boo's locket showed streamers streaming and confetti popping.

The girls gasped. They had no idea it was Aurora's birthday!

Canterpop smiled. "Whenever there's a special occasion in Enchanted Valley, I think up the best way to celebrate it. Every year, Queen Aurora tells me she doesn't want a fuss for her birthday – but

I know all Aurora's friends would love to celebrate with her. So, triplets," Canterpop said, "will you tell the girls your plan?"

"We're going to throw Aurora a party!" cried Bunting.

"A surprise party with lots of surprises!" said Boo. Her eyes shone. "Surprises are the best!"

"And there'll be lots of presents," added Boxie.

"And amazing decorations," said Bunting.

Emily and Aisha grinned. "It sounds brilliant!" said Emily.

"It's why I called you to Enchanted Valley," explained Canterpop.

"You called us here?" asked Aisha.

"Not Queen Aurora?" said Emily.

"Yes!" said Canterpop. "Would you like to help with the party?"

Delight bubbled through the girls like lemonade. "We'd love to!" they said together.

"Now for the first part of the plan!" said Canterpop. "Wait here, everyone."

Aisha, Emily and the unicorn triplets watched through the branches of the willow tree as Canterpop walked up to the palace drawbridge and tapped her front hoof against the door. "Queen Aurora?" she called. "Are you home?"

After a little while, a beautiful unicorn trotted out of the palace. As usual, she was a shimmering mix of red, pink, orange

and gold – all the colours of a beautiful
sunrise. But today, her long mane was
twirled up in curlers and she wore a green
dressing gown with a frilly collar draped
over her back. It was Queen Aurora!
Emily and Aisha smiled at each other –
they were always glad to see Enchanted
Valley's clever and gentle ruler, but they
had never seen her in her dressing gown
before!

"Oh, I'm sorry to disturb you, Your
Majesty," said Canterpop. "Were you
asleep?"

"That's quite all right," said Queen
Aurora. Her voice was rich and warm.
"I was just styling my mane." Her eyes
twinkled. "Let me guess – you've come to

ask about my birthday, haven't you?"

Canterpop shook her head. "I know you won't want to celebrate it," she said. "I've actually come to invite you to visit our friend Twinkleangelo with me."

"Twinkleangelo?" Queen Aurora tossed her elegant horn in delight. "I've not seen him for ages!"

Aisha turned to the unicorn triplets, who were pressed up against the girls under the tree. "Who's Twinkleangelo?" she whispered.

"He's a painter," whispered Boxie.

"The best painter in Enchanted Valley," said Bunting.

"And Aurora's friend," added Boo.

Queen Aurora tilted her head

thoughtfully. "But I'm not sure I should leave the palace. What if Selena tries another of her wicked plots?"

"No one's seen her for a while now," said Canterpop. "She won't even know you've gone away."

Queen Aurora looked deep in thought for a few moments.

"Please say yes …" Bunting whispered to himself. "Our plan won't work otherwise!"

Then Queen Aurora smiled. "Very well," she said. "Let's go. After all, it would be very, very unlucky for Selena to turn up when I'm away for one night." Her horn glowed, and golden sparkles swirled around it. Her dressing gown vanished, and then her curlers did too, leaving her mane tumbling around her neck in soft waves. "Now I'm ready," she said. "Off we go!"

Also available

Book One:

Book Two:

Book Three:

Book Four:

Look out for the next book!

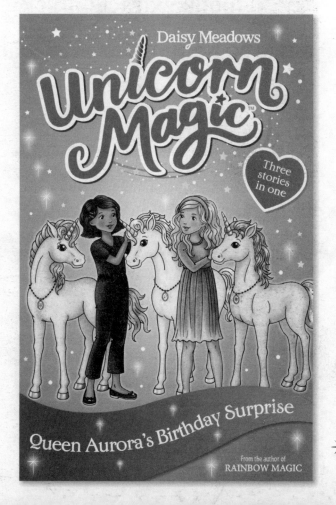

Daisy Meadows

Unicorn Magic™

Three stories in one

Queen Aurora's Birthday Surprise

From the author of
RAINBOW MAGIC

Visit
orchardseriesbooks.co.uk
for

* ✶ fun activities ✶
* ✶ exclusive content ✶
* ✶ book extracts ✶

There's something for everyone!